DODOS ARE FOREVER

The dodos were happily leading idyllic lives on a smallish island in the middle of the Indian Ocean. The date was AD 1650 and soon (though luckily the dodos weren't to know this), there would be no dodos anywhere at all on earth. The dodos would become extinct—or so everyone thought. Beatrice and Bertie were joyously planning their wedded bliss and thinking of the dodolings they would produce, unaware of the dangers lurking off-shore in the anchored ship. The sea-monkeys and rats on board were dangerous and hungry—and the poor unsuspecting dodos were in trouble!

DODOS
ARE FOREVER

Dick King-Smith

Illustrated by David Parkins

A Lythway Book

CHIVERS PRESS
BATH

CONTENTS

CHAPTER ONE

A PROPOSAL

'Oh, Beatrice!' cried Bertie. 'You are, beyond doubt, the most beautiful dodo in the whole wide world.'

The whole wide world was, for the dodos (though they did not know this), a smallish island in the middle of the Indian Ocean. There were no dodos anywhere else on earth.

The date (though they did not know this) was AD 1650, and before very long (and, luckily, they did not know this either) there would be no dodos anywhere at all on earth. The dodo would be extinct.

Or that's what everybody has always thought.

Till now.

* * *

Beatrice bridled with pleasure at her boyfriend's words. She bent her neck,

1

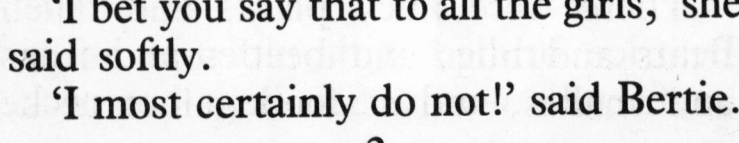

for she was somewhat larger than him, and scratched the top of his head with the hooked point of her long, oddly shaped beak.

'I bet you say that to all the girls,' she said softly.

'I most certainly do not!' said Bertie.

He looked around at the rest of the huge flock of dodos feeding busily along the shore, tearing open crabs and other shellfish with their tin-opener bills. 'It wouldn't worry me,' he said, 'if all that lot was wiped out, so long as I still had you.'

'Silly!' said Beatrice fondly. 'And, anyway, they couldn't possibly be wiped out. Dodos have no enemies; everyone knows that.'

And at the time, she was right.

For tens of thousands of years dodos had lived happily on that island—and died too, but usually of old age. With their huge bodies and their stupid little wings, they could not possibly fly like other birds. But this did not worry them, because they had never flown. Heavy, awkward and clumsy, they could not run much either. But this did not worry them as there was nothing to run away from, and as for running after things, there was no need. The island was always full of dodo food.

There were juicy plants and fallen fruits and bugs and beetles and frogs and snakes, and seafood galore to be caught off the coast of the island.

Beatrice and Bertie walked ponderously down the beach to the sea, making their way through the throng of dodos—huge hens, slightly smaller cock birds and gangs of little dodolings—who walked or played, or simply sat and sunbathed on the golden sands.

The day was beautifully hot, the sea-breeze refreshing, and the waves sparkled and glinted and glittered all the way to the far horizon.

Bertie cleared his throat. 'H'm,' he said. 'Very pleasant weather for the time of year.'

'Silly!' said Beatrice. 'It's always very pleasant weather here, whatever the time of year.'

She waded in a little way, Bertie following, and they stood side by side and looked out to sea, enjoying the feeling of the warm water swirling round their large feet.

'This is an earthly paradise,' she said. 'As it always has been for our ancestors since time began.'

'And will be for our children,' said

Bertie daringly. 'Sure as eggs is eggs.'

'Oh, Bertie!' said Beatrice. 'You are a caution!' and she gave him a playful nudge that made him stagger.

Bertie righted himself and moved a little closer to Beatrice, so that one of his stubby, useless wings touched hers. He cleared his throat again. 'Beatrice,' he said.

'Yes, Bertie?'

'I was wondering...'

'Yes, Bertie?'

'Oh, dash it all!' said Bertie. 'What I mean is ... it would make me the happiest dodo in the world...'

'Yes, Bertie?'

'...If you would marry me.'

'Yes, Bertie.'

Bertie gulped. 'You mean you will?' he said.

Beatrice did not answer, and Bertie, shooting a sideways glance at her, saw that she was staring out to sea towards the horizon that had been empty when they began their paddle, but was empty no longer. Sailing towards them (though neither dodo knew what they were looking at, never having seen such a thing before) was a large ship.

'What is that?' said Beatrice.

'I have no idea,' said Bertie. 'But it cannot concern us. You have not answered my question, Beatrice. Will you marry me?'

'Of course, Bertie darling,' said Beatrice, 'and we will live happily ever after.' They stood wing to wing, watching placidly as the great ship drew nearer to the shore.

CHAPTER TWO

A DEATH

At the rattle of the anchor-chain, all the adult dodos stopped whatever they were doing to stand and stare seawards. Only the dodolings, regardless of their doom, continued to sport upon the shore, towards which there now came what looked like two giant water-beetles, sculling across the waves.

Beatrice and Bertie and all their companions watched in astonishment as the sailors beached their boats and, leaping out, dragged them up on to the sands.

'Look, Bertie!' said Beatrice. 'What strange birds are these? They have no feathers, no beaks to speak of, and the oddest wings.'

Bertie had never set eyes on a human being, but there were monkeys on the island, and he had often seen them stand up on their hindlegs and chatter away, just as these creatures were doing.

'These are not birds,' he said in a knowledgeable voice. 'These are giant monkeys.'

'Monkeys?' said Beatrice. 'From the sea?'

'Sea-monkeys,' said Bertie firmly.

'They are very excitable, certainly,' said Beatrice, and, indeed, the sailors were as happy as sand-boys at finding themselves on dry land again after many months at sea. For a long time now their only food had been salted beef and hard, weevily ship's biscuits, their only drink water so long in the cask that it was more like a thick green soup alive with wriggling things.

The first thought in their heads was of fresh, cool, clean water, and when they found a stream at the head of the beach, they threw themselves down beside it and drank till it seemed they would burst. Some then set about filling the water-casks that they had brought from the ship, while others began to explore. They found all kinds of fruits and wolfed them down, and they shook down coconuts which they

split open with their cutlasses.

Only when all had eaten and drunk their fill did the sailors really take much notice of the dodos. At first they did no more than stand and point and laugh amongst themselves at the sight of all those huge clumsy birds who waddled trustingly about, squawking to one another in low voices.

Two of Beatrice and Bertie's friends

came up. They were a young married couple named Fatima and Felix, and the four of them spent much time together, foraging for food or sun-bathing or simply in conversation.

The two couples touched beaks now in the usual dodo greeting, and then Felix said, 'Bertie, old boy, what on earth are these strange creatures?'

'Yes, whatever are they, Beatrice?' asked Fatima. 'Do you know?'

'They're sea-monkeys,' said Beatrice.

'Sea-monkeys?'

'Yes. That's what Bertie says.'

Bertie looked knowing.

'But shall I tell you something far more important that Bertie has just said?' cried Beatrice. 'Or rather, something he has just asked me.'

Bertie looked smug.

'What?' said Fatima and Felix.

'Bertie,' said Beatrice, 'has just asked me to marry him. We are engaged!'

'Oh, Beatrice!' cried Fatima. 'How lovely!'

'Congratulations, Bertie old boy!' said Felix. 'You're a lucky dodo.' But then, before anyone could say anything else, they were almost knocked off their feet by a stampede of dodos, who were squawking with fright. Behind them came the sailors, standing and staring no longer but running. Some carried cutlasses and some stout sticks, and they were gaining rapidly on the fattest and slowest birds.

Beatrice and Bertie and their two friends took to their heels and ran away as fast as they could go, not stopping until they were deep in among the trees and could hear no sound of pursuit.

'Oh, Bertie!' panted Beatrice. 'Whatever were those sea-monkeys playing at?'

The answer would have been plain, had they ventured back to the shore that evening.

A great fire of driftwood blazed upon the beach, a fire on which the sailors were cooking their supper, and the smell of that supper was borne on the sea-breeze. How rich and appetizing it was, and how the sailors' mouths watered! It was the smell of roast dodo.

13

CHAPTER THREE

AN AUNT

By the following morning most of the dodos had practically forgotten about the incidents of the previous day, and came out of the shelter of the trees early to comb the beach, as was their habit. Scavenging was part of their way of life, and each day the Indian Ocean threw up all manner of interesting items of food—dead flesh, dead fish, including good dead red herring.

The circle of grey ashes on the golden sands meant nothing to them, nor the vague lingering scent of roasted meat, for like most birds, their sense of smell was so poor as to be non-existent. If they did notice a large pile of feathers near the site of the fire, or a number of bones lying about, they did not put two and two together.

Even the sight of the ship riding at anchor on the swell did not disturb them, so secure did they still feel in the

14

peace and tranquillity of their earthly paradise.

Bertie and Beatrice, and their friends Felix and Fatima, came late to the beach. Thoughtful by nature, more intelligent perhaps than the average dodo, they had spent some time in discussion before setting out for the morning's foraging. The fact that Bertie, and Bertie alone, had actually known the identity of the creatures that had landed on their island impressed the others.

'Those sea-monkeys,' said Beatrice. 'Had you ever seen them before, Bertie dear?'

'Never,' said Bertie truthfully.

'Yet you knew straight away what they were, didn't you, old boy?' said Felix.

'Of course,' lied Bertie.

'But why were they chasing us, Bertie?' asked Fatima. 'Surely not to hurt us? Dodos have no enemies, everyone knows that.'

'High spirits,' said Bertie. 'Sea-monkeys are just like the rest of that family—excitable, aimless, foolish beasts. I cannot think why you all ran away.'

'You ran too,' they all said.

'I was carried along in the crush,' said Bertie.

'Well, I know why I ran,' said Beatrice. 'I was frightened.'

'So was I,' said Fatima.

'Me too,' admitted Felix.

The three of them looked inquiringly at Bertie.

'Oh, very well,' he said in a grumpy voice. 'Yes, I was scared too. But it'll be all right now. The sea-monkeys will have gone.'

I hope, he thought.

And, sure enough, there were no sea-monkeys on the beach when they reached it, but just the usual flock of foraging dodos.

The four birds were drinking at the stream in typical dodo fashion, walking backwards with bent heads and scooping water into their huge curved beaks, when suddenly Bertie heard his name called. Coming towards them was a middle-aged female dodo, who appeared to be very agitated. Her beak

16

hung open in distress, and the candyfloss plume of feathers that every dodo displayed jauntily on its fat backside was jaunty no longer, but drooped in a melancholy manner.

'Bertie!' cried the bird again mournfully. 'Have you seen him?'

'Why,' said Bertie as she drew near, 'it's Aunt Florence! Whatever's the matter, Aunty? Have I seen who?'

'Your uncle,' panted Aunt Florence. 'I can't find him anywhere. I've searched, I've asked, but no one seems to have seen your Uncle Eric. I lost touch with him yesterday afternoon when everyone was rushing about in that silly way. He can't run very fast, you will remember, because of his accident.'

Bertie's Uncle Eric had indeed lost two of his three front toes in an unfortunate encounter with a giant clam that had closed upon his foot while he was foraging in the shallows. So fierce was the clam's grip that two toes had been severed.

'He didn't come home to roost last night,' said Aunt Florence. 'In fact, your Uncle Eric seems to have disappeared from the face of the island.'

'Don't worry, Aunty,' said Bertie, 'I'm sure he's around somewhere. Felix and I will undertake a thorough search. You sit here and rest awhile.'

'Yes,' said Beatrice. 'Have a nice long drink to calm you.'

'And we will fetch you some food,' said Fatima.

Bertie and Felix set out to look for the missing uncle, and on their way they passed the site of the fire.

'What are those bones?' said Bertie.

'And what are those feathers?' said Felix.

At that moment the sea-breeze lifted the pile of feathers and scattered them. The two friends could now see a curious-looking object. They examined it. It was the foot of a dodo, a foot that had only one front toe.

'Upon my soul!' cried Bertie. 'My uncle!'

'Alas, poor Eric!' said Felix. 'I knew him, Bertie.' He shook his head in disbelief that such a thing could have happened. 'Shall we ever know the inside story?' he said.

'Uncle Eric's inside the sea-monkeys,' said Bertie. 'That's the story.'

'Did you know that sea-monkeys ate dodos?' asked Felix.

'No,' said Bertie truthfully.

Felix stared out towards the ship. 'Do you think they'll come again?' he said.

'No,' lied Bertie.

Whatever are we to do, he thought. If those sea-monkeys liked the taste of Uncle Eric, they'll be back for a second helping.

'Aunt Florence must never know,' said Bertie. 'The shock would kill her.'

'That might be a more merciful death,' said Felix drily. 'Look!'

From the ship the two giant water-beetles came sculling once more towards the shore.

CHAPTER FOUR

A MASSACRE

'Take cover!' cried Bertie.

Peering out from the shelter of the trees that fringed the shore, they watched as the sailors beached their boats once again and clambered out. This time they did not dash about excitedly or make any attempt to chase the dodos that were on the sands, but instead began to walk slowly and quietly among them. All the birds, even the dodolings, stood still and looked calmly at them.

One of the sea-monkeys, Bertie and Felix observed, seemed to be the leader. He wore a strange thing on his head (they knew nothing of hats in general, let alone cocked hats), and he strode ahead of the others. On his shoulder sat a green parrot.

'They seem quiet enough this time,' said Felix. 'Perhaps they did not mean to kill your Uncle Eric. Maybe the

excitement brought on a heart attack and he just dropped dead.'

'And plucked himself and cooked himself, I suppose,' said Bertie sardonically.

Hardly were the words out of his beak when the leader stopped and pointed at the nearest dodo. Immediately a sea-monkey produced a heavy cudgel and struck the bird upon the head. It slumped lifeless to the sand, and the green parrot let out a loud scream.

Horror-struck and hypnotized, Bertie and Felix watched as time after time the sea-monkeys' leader pointed, the cudgel was raised, and another scream told of another death.

*   *   *

'Tasted like chicken, did it?' the captain of the ship had said when the sailors returned from the first landing. 'Then I'll tell you what, my hearties. Tomorrow we'll go ashore and help ourselves to a feast. What we can't eat straight off, we'll salt down and store in the beef casks, and I'll have the plumage off of 'em to make me a fine feather bed. We'll have a couple of dozen of the fattest to begin with, what say you, my lads?'

'Aye, aye, sir!' roared the sailors, and 'Aye, aye, sir!' screamed the parrot perched on the captain's shoulder.

*   *   *

Twenty-four times in all did the parrot scream that morning, while Bertie and Felix watched helplessly, and the other dodos stood and stared stupidly as the bodies of their companions were loaded into the boats. The day had begun bright and blowy, but now the breeze had dropped away to nothing and the blue of the sky turned to a brassy glare. Then, suddenly, as though in mourning for the massacre of the dodos, a pall of ominous black cloud appeared on the horizon and in the stillness could be heard a far-distant sound, a kind of whining moan.

Hardly had the rowing-boats reached the ship and been hauled aboard than the darkened surface of the sea began to heave and slide. In it, swimming madly shoreward, was a little host of furry grey shapes. The rats had abandoned ship.

Now the distant moaning seemed nearer, and was becoming louder and shriller. Then the watching dodos saw far out at sea a great white wall of water coming towards the ship, towards the land, towards them, at breakneck speed.

Beatrice and Fatima were sitting by the stream comforting Aunt Florence with a light meal of shrimps, when Bertie and Felix ran (that is to say, waddled as fast as they could) towards them.

'Quickly!' cried Bertie. 'To high ground, all of you, quickly!' Behind him the typhoon burst upon the island.

* * *

The tidal wave swept the beach clean, and washed over all but the higher parts of the island. It rolled away again across the ocean, while the wind that followed it howled like all the devils in hell. Hurtling helplessly along in its grip came a host of small songbirds and even a number of dodolings, airborne for the first and only time in their lives.

The force of the typhoon plucked the very palm trees from the ground, and filled the air with their branches and fronds and a fusillade of falling coconuts that rained down like cannon-balls.

One of these struck Aunt Florence upon the head. It was a glancing blow, not to be compared with the cudgel-stroke of a sea-monkey, but it knocked her cold.

Bertie and the others huddled together, blinded by blown sand and spray, buffeted by flying debris, deafened by the yell of the storm, while for hours, it seemed (it was really minutes), the typhoon shook the island as a dog shakes a rat. Then it was gone.

Afterwards the four of them could remember nothing of its fury, so stupefied with fear had they been. As for Aunt Florence, she could remember nothing about anything.

'Aunty! Aunty!' cried Bertie anxiously when they found her prostrate form. 'Speak to me, Aunty!'

After a moment Aunt Florence opened her eyes and looked at him. 'I do not think that we have been introduced', she said.

'I'm Bertie!' said Bertie. 'Don't you remember me?'

'Bertie?' said Aunt Florence. 'I know

no one by that name.'

'But I'm your nephew!'

Aunt Florence rose to her feet. 'How very nice!' she said pleasantly. 'I have always wanted a nephew. How do you do?'

The others looked at one another. Then they looked at the large coconut lying near by. Then they looked at the egg-shaped bump on the back of Aunt Florence's head.

'Lost her memory,' said Bertie in a low voice.

'Just as well,' said Felix.

'Why?' said Beatrice and Fatima.

'Because she's lost her husband, too,' said Bertie, and he told them of the sad end of his uncle, and of the massacre of the dodos that had occurred that morning.

'How dreadful!' cried Beatrice. 'At least Aunt Florence has escaped such a fate. Better to be widowed than dead.'

'I suppose,' said Fatima doubtfully.

'Try her with her husband's name, Bertie,' said Beatrice. 'She doesn't recognize you, but surely she will remember him.'

'Aunty,' said Bertie, 'do you know anyone called Eric?'

'No, I'm thankful to say,' replied his aunt. 'Not a name I care for at all. And now let us go to the beach and find something to eat. I'm hungry.'

When at last the five dodos reached the beach, after picking their way through a tangle of fallen palm trees, Felix and Fatima set off in one direction, Aunt Florence in another. Bertie and Beatrice stood wing to wing and surveyed the scene. The shore was empty of life. Even the gulls seemed to have been blown away by the typhoon, and as for the ship, there was no sign of it.

'It's an ill wind that blows nobody any good,' said Beatrice. 'At least those horrible sea-monkeys have gone.' Then they both jumped at the sound of a sudden loud harsh voice.

'Ahoy there, me hearties!' shouted the same voice, and turning, they saw a green parrot walking towards them with a rolling sailor's gait. When it reached them, it stood and looked up at them with a bright considering eye.

'Blow me down and shiver me timbers!' it said, rather more quietly. 'Sailed the seven seas I have, and never till today clapped eyes on such birds as you! Tell me, landlubbers—what do they call you?'

'We are dodos,' said Bertie. 'My name is Bertie, and this is my fiancée, Beatrice. Who are you?'

'Drake's the name,' said the green parrot.

'Drake?'

'Francis Drake. *Sir* Francis Drake, to give me my full title, but I'm not fussy about that.'

'Sir Francis Drake,' said Bertie, wondering. 'That's the finest of names.'

'I'm called after the finest of sailors,' said the parrot.

'Sailors? What are sailors?'

'They go down to the sea in ships, that do business in great waters,' said the parrot, 'and some pretty dirty business on dry land too, as you'll have seen this day.'

'Oh, you mean the sea-monkeys,' said Bertie. 'It was you sitting on the shoulder of their leader, was it?'

Sir Francis Drake let out a screech of laughter. 'Sea-monkeys, eh?' he said. 'Is that what you call them? Well, you needn't worry about those ones. You've nothing to fear from them.'

'Why not?' asked Beatrice.

'Because they've all gone to Davy Jones's locker.'

'I don't understand,' said Bertie.

'It's simple,' said Sir Francis. 'Food for the fish, that's what your sea-monkeys are.'

'Might not some have swum ashore?' said Beatrice.

'Sharks,' said the parrot shortly.

'Sailormen,' he went on, 'are clever creatures. They can reef and steer, splice a rope and box the compass, and run aloft in the rigging like the monkeys you think they are. But when the ship goes down, down go the sailors. Down to the bottom of the deep blue sea. Full fathom five my captain lies. Bigger and stronger and cleverer than this old parrot he might have been, but when the typhoon struck, there was just one thing I could do that he couldn't.'

'What was that?' said Bertie.

'Fly,' said Sir Francis Drake.

'It would be nice to fly,' said Beatrice wistfully. 'I wish I could. It looks so graceful.'

The parrot began a shriek of mirth at the thought of big fat Beatrice flying, but managed to turn it into a kind of admiring whistle.

'You could not possibly look more graceful than you do, my love,' said Bertie gallantly.

'Silly!' said Beatrice fondly, and she gave him a nudge that made him stagger.

'You're a lucky dog, Bertie,' said the parrot straight faced, 'to be marrying such an elegant young lady.'

'Why, thank you . . . er, um . . .' said Bertie.

'Oh, you are a one, Sir . . . um, er . . .' giggled Beatrice.

'Call me Frank,' said Sir Francis Drake. 'Frank by name and frank by nature, that's me. And I'll tell you something, you two, because I like the cut of your jib. Sooner or later another ship will call here, and next time there's

not likely to be a typhoon to save your skins. Next time the sea-monkeys will finish you all off. They're like that. They'll kill every last one of you, you mark my words. And when the last one dies, why, the race will be extinct.'

'The dodo extinct!' cried Beatrice. 'Surely not!'

'You must be joking, Frank,' said Bertie. 'Dodos are forever.'

CHAPTER FIVE

A WEDDING

For several days after the storm the surviving dodos on the island had been in a state of shock. Many lives had been lost. There was hardly a bird that was not in mourning for some relative, slain by the sea-monkeys or drowned by the tidal wave, and morale was very low. Only Aunt Florence was perfectly happy, since she didn't remember anything.

So many long faces got on Sir Francis's nerves. 'A castaway I may be,' he said to Bertie and the others, 'but I wouldn't mind a bit of a laugh now and again. 'Tis time we had a bit of fun, me hearties—time to splice the main brace, set to partners and dance and skylark. Eat, drink and be merry, for tomorrow . . .' he stopped suddenly.

'Tomorrow what, Frank?' asked Bertie.

Sir Francis Drake looked at Bertie

and Beatrice, and had a sudden good idea. 'Tomorrow,' he said, 'we'll have a wedding and invite all the dodos, and everyone will forget their troubles. And as for you two, why, may all your troubles be little ones!'

'Oh, Frank!' cried Beatrice. 'You are a caution!' She tried to give the parrot one of her nudges, but he hopped smartly out of the way.

And what a wedding feast it was!

Once the news spread everyone became very excited, and eagerly began to collect supplies of choice food—the finest fruit, the plumpest and most succulent of shellfish—and to carry in coconuts and crack them open to provide the drinks. Sir Francis sampled some coconut milk.

Refreshing, he said to himself, though I'd sooner have a tot of rum.

The wedding day dawned warm and bright as usual, and, with the exception of those hen birds who were sitting on eggs, every dodo on the island turned up to attend the ceremony. It was conducted by Sir Francis Drake. ('A ship's captain can perform a marriage,' said he, 'so there's no doubt that an admiral can.') Felix was best man and Fatima the matron of honour.

Everyone had a splendid time and, as Sir Francis had predicted, they forgot all about their worries, especially Aunt Florence who, having forgotten everything, had nothing to worry about anyway. She in fact became so intoxicated by the party spirit (and maybe a little too much coconut milk, slightly fermented by the hot sun) that she had to lean upon the wing of a total stranger, an elderly but well-preserved cock dodo named Hugo from another part of the island. They were still together, Beatrice noticed, when she and Bertie set off for their honeymoon on a distant beach.

* * *

Many weeks had passed since then and when Bertie asked his wife whether she was happy, there was only one possible answer. 'Oh, Bertie, you are a silly! Of course I am!'

Quite apart from wedded bliss,

happiness was in fact the normal state of the dodos. Living—usually to a great age—in an almost perfect climate, with ample food and without enemies, no dodo had ever had cause for unhappiness. Until the coming of the sea-monkeys, that is. But thanks to short memories, the excitement of the wedding feast, and the influence of the ever-cheerful Sir Francis Drake, no one now gave a thought to those terrible creatures. They had sunk to the bottom of the sea and the bottom of the dodos' minds. What they had also forgotten, however, was that Sir Francis had not been the only one to escape the wreck.

Even now, as Beatrice and Bertie walked and talked upon the beach, sharp eyes were watching them from cover, and sharp noses with twitching whiskers were lifted. Maybe a score of rats had swum ashore from the ship, but by now there were ten times that number on the island, so fast had they bred.

Rats eat anything and everything, and there was plenty of food for them. But, in addition, they soon discovered there was a supply of delicacies—dodo eggs!

Above all things rats love to eat eggs, and when the castaways first chanced upon the egg of a dodo, their sharp eyes nearly jumped out of their heads with surprise and delight, so large was it. A single rat could not have broken it open, could hardly have moved it, indeed; but a number of them set upon it, and pushed it about until it rolled against a jagged stone. Once it cracked,

they shoved their pointed noses into it and gorged themselves.

Already—though the dodos did not realize it—the rats were as great a danger as the sea-monkeys had been. The hen dodo doesn't make a proper nest for the single egg that she lays, but simply drops it in any place that takes her fancy, such as a sandy depression or a grassy hollow. And, being slow of thought and movement, she may well decide not to sit upon it straight away. She is in no rush to begin six weeks of squatting in the heat of the day and the chill of the night, with the great egg pressed against the bare brood-patch in the middle of her fat stomach, a stomach which her mate must work hard to fill throughout the long incubation. No hurry, she thinks. Plenty of time. And off she goes, leaving plenty of time for the rats.

All over the place there were hen birds coming back to the spot where they had left their egg, finding nothing there, and deciding in a puzzled way that perhaps they hadn't laid one after all.

Now the rats had taken to following individual dodos around, and a gang of them were watching Beatrice. It was the bigger dodos, they had already learned, who laid eggs. They posed no threat to the birds themselves—one tap of those nutcracker beaks would have split a rat's skull—but they would have licked their lips if they could have understood what Beatrice said next.

★ ★ ★

'And talking of happiness, Bertie dear,' she said, 'could you be happier than you are?'

'Not possibly,' said Bertie.

'Can't you think of anything that would make life even more wonderful?'

'No,' said Bertie.

'Not even if I said I had something to tell you? A little secret?'

'I don't follow you,' said Bertie.

'Daddy!' said Beatrice coyly.

Bertie's beak fell open. 'You mean . . .' he said.

'Yes, dearest,' said Beatrice. 'I'm going to have an egg.'

CHAPTER SIX

AN EGG

'When?' asked Bertie.

'Any minute now, by the feel of things,' said Beatrice.

Bertie looked wildly around. He did not see the skulking rats, but what he did see was a number of family parties of dodos on the beach. The parents were taking their ease in the sunshine while their dodolings played games on the sands.

'You cannot do it in public!' he said.

'I don't see why not.' said Beatrice. 'It's perfectly natural.' But Bertie could not bear the thought of his child—or what was to become his child—being born in front of a lot of strangers, so he hurried Beatrice away into the shelter of the trees that fringed the beach. Half a dozen low grey shapes crept after them, their long naked tails dragging along the ground. They watched unseen as Beatrice found a convenient

41

hollow and squatted in it.

Bertie fussed around as fathers-to-be do, striding up and down, balancing first on one foot and then the other, unable to keep still for a second. Then Beatrice gave a kind of grunt and stood up.

There on the ground Bertie could see a huge, glistening, new-laid egg, its pearly-white shell laced and dotted with rust-red speckles. He had seen hundreds of dodo eggs in his time, but this one was without doubt the finest.

'Oh, Beatrice, my love!' cried Bertie. 'It's beautiful!'

'It is,' said Beatrice, 'though I say so myself.'

'Our baby!' breathed Bertie.

'Well, not quite,' said Beatrice, 'there's still a long way to go. And before I start sitting, I could do with a good square meal. The effort has made me quite peckish.'

'You mean . . . leave him . . . her . . . it here, alone?' said Bertie.

'Why ever not, silly?' said Beatrice. 'It'll come to no harm.' She walked away towards the beach, Bertie following.

As they neared it, a familiar voice cried 'Ahoy!' from a tree. Looking up, they saw Sir Francis Drake.

'How's life then, my friends?' he said. 'All shipshape and Bristol fashion?'

'Guess what, Frank,' said Bertie excitedly. 'Beatrice has just laid an egg!'

'Where?' said Sir Francis sharply.

'Just a little way back there, in among the trees,' said Bertie. 'You can't miss it. It's a beautiful colour, all speckly, isn't it, dearest? We'll show it to you later, Frank.' But then he realized that the parrot had flown off at top speed in the direction from which they had come.

'Well, I must say,' grumbled Bertie, 'that's rather rude. He didn't even say congratulations.'

'I don't suppose it means much to him,' said Beatrice, but she sounded a little hurt.

★　　★　　★

43

The moment the dodos were out of sight, the rats had acted. These were no ordinary rats. Their leader was a fat old female, and she was the first to have found, and, with the help of her five sons, to have broken into and eaten a dodo's egg soon after the typhoon. Since then she had trained her sons into a ruthlessly efficient team, and because of their success and thus the richness of their diet, they had all grown unusually large and strong. The old doe herself was the biggest and most cunning rat on the island. Her name was Lucrezia Gorger. It suited her for she was very greedy, always gorging herself to bursting point.

Now the five Gorger boys formed up behind Beatrice's egg and set their snouts against it, while their mother urged them on.

'Heave, my sons!' squealed Lucrezia. 'This way! All together now!' She began to manoeuvre a sharp-edged stone into the path of the rolling egg. The last thing any of them was expecting was a furious airborne attack.

The moment he'd heard that Beatrice had laid her egg, Sir Francis Drake knew that there was no time to lose. The dodos may have been unaware of the havoc that the rats were beginning to cause on the island, but the parrot knew well enough. He had seen the vandals at work as he flew about. He did not doubt that Beatrice's egg might already be in great danger.

Sir Francis knew all about rats from his many years at sea. He had seen them running along the mooring-ropes to board a ship or to leave it at another port of call. He knew what damage they did to stores of food in the hold of a ship or even in the galley, where they would steal from under the cook's nose. (And not only did they eat, they were eaten, for he had seen more than one hungry sailor make a good meal of a biscuit-fattened rat.) He knew also that they were by nature cowardly creatures, and when he sighted these ones already attacking Beatrice's egg, it did not occur to him for one moment that they would put up a fight.

Surprise, the little admiral knew, was a valuable weapon, and he flew silently, giving no warning of his approach until he was almost upon them. Only then did he blast them with a sudden fusillade of words.

'All hands on deck!' shouted Sir Francis Drake at the top of his voice as he swooped upon the Gorgers. 'Stand by to repel boarders! Pikes and cutlasses, my lads! Give them a taste of cold steel!'

At this tirade the five young bucks left the egg and fled, but Lucrezia was made of sterner stuff. She leaped at Sir Francis as he landed and fastened her yellow teeth in his leg. She was as big and as heavy as him, and though the parrot set to work with his hooked bill, things might have gone badly for him had not Beatrice and Bertie, attracted by the row, come galumphing through the trees. On sight of them, Lucrezia Gorger loosed her grip and scuttled away.

'Whatever is happening?' cried the dodos. They then listened in horror as

Sir Francis told them what had occurred.

'Another few moments,' he said, 'and those pirates would have had your egg for breakfast!'

'Frank, old fellow,' said Bertie gruffly. 'You saved our child! How can we ever thank you?'

'And your poor leg is bleeding, Frank dear,' said Beatrice.

"'Tis nothing,' said Sir Francis Drake. 'Naught but a scratch to an old sea-dog like me, but a scratch that that great ugly rat shall pay for dearly, mark my words. As for you, my friends, be warned. If you want to hatch this egg, it mustn't be left unprotected from this moment. You must sit upon it now, Beatrice, and you and me, Bertie, must stand guard, watch and watch about, until the child is born.'

So, without further ado, Beatrice settled upon the egg. Bertie marched round and round her, working himself up into a fine fury at the thought of the rats and their villainy, while Sir Francis flew off to the sea to bathe his leg in salt water.

In the bushes not far away, Lucrezia Gorger sat and swore at him. 'Screeching, squawking devil!' she growled. 'What business is it of his which egg we take?'

'We can't get it now, Ma,' said one of the Gorger boys. 'The big bird's sitting on it. Let's find another. There are plenty about.'

'Shut your trap, boy!' said his

mother. 'I fancy this egg, if only to spite that cursed parrot.'

She licked at the wounds that Sir Francis's beak had inflicted and her beady eyes glinted with fury. 'Next time it'll not be his leg that I sink my teeth into. It'll be his throat!' snarled Lucrezia Gorger.

CHAPTER SEVEN

A BIRTH

'Reinforcements!' said Sir Francis Drake to himself as he paddled cautiously (for like many sailors, he could not swim) at the very edge of the ripples. He flew off, humming a sea-shanty, to find Felix and Fatima.

No help, however, was to be forthcoming from this quarter, as Fatima was to lay an egg very shortly. So, after warning them most earnestly of the danger of rats, Sir Francis flew on in search of Aunt Florence.

He found her in the company of the elderly but well-preserved Hugo. They were standing wing to wing, as courting couples do, and though dodos' faces show little expression, the parrot thought that they looked the picture of contentment. He landed before them and hobbled up to address Aunt Florence.

'Good day, ma'am,' he said. 'I don't

know if you remember me?'

'Sir Francis!' cried Aunt Florence with a light laugh. 'How nice to see you again. Of course I remember you! Why, anyone would think that I had lost my memory!' and she laughed again, heartily now.

What a merry widow she is, thought Sir Francis. He caught Hugo's eye, but it was blank. Just as well, he thought. He knows no more of her past than she does. Poor Uncle Eric, He would turn in his grave, if he'd had one.

Aunt Florence turned to her slightly smaller companion. 'Hugo,' she said, 'allow me to introduce Sir Francis Drake. Sir Francis is a friend of my new-found nephew, Bertie.'

'I am honoured to make your acquaintance, Sir,' said Hugo, and he bowed his head till the tip of his beak touched the ground.

Taken aback by so courtly a gesture, Sir Francis replied, 'Your servant, Sir.' He made to bend a polite knee, but the effort so hurt his injured leg that he had hastily to stifle a rude sailorman's oath.

'It is on behalf of Bertie and

Beatrice,' he said, 'that I come to see you, ma'am...'

'Oh, do please call me Florence!'

'...To seek your assistance.'

'Assistance? I trust that they are not in any trouble, Sir Francis?'

'Oh, do please call me Frank!'

'Must I? "Sir Francis" has such a ring to it!'

'Oh, just as you like,' said the parrot a trifle testily. He was becoming extremely anxious to get back to the nest-site before night should fall with its usual tropical suddenness, so he outlined the position bluntly and briefly.

'So you see,' he concluded, 'that if Beatrice and Bertie's egg is to be saved, we need all the help we can get. Will you come?'

'Of course!' said Aunt Florence. 'To think, it will be my great-niece or great-nephew! Just let those rats show their faces, eh, Hugo? We'll teach them!'

Hugo stiffened his rather rounded shoulders and puffed out his rather narrow chest. 'Once more into the breach, dear friends, once more,' he cried. 'Or close the nest up with our dodo dead.'

What an old actor! thought Sir Francis as he flew back at top speed. Anyone would suppose they were guarding Beatrice against a pack of ravening wolves instead of a few ordinary rats. But one of these rats, as he was reminded when he jarred his leg on landing, was extraordinary, and it

was with great relief that he found Beatrice sitting placidly, with Bertie at attention by her side.

'They've gone, Frank!' he cried. 'The rats have gone!'

★   ★   ★

From her place of concealment, Lucrezia Gorger watched the parrot arrive and saw, a little later, two more dodos come lumbering through the trees.

She had dismissed her five sons, telling them to walk openly past the nest and away. She was confident that the dodos would not know the exact number of the team, and, seeing the exodus, would perhaps relax their guard and once more leave the egg unprotected. How she then alone would break it, she did not know, but perhaps she could roll it away and hide it somewhere.

But now, watching the reinforcements arrive, she knew there was nothing more to be attempted till the morrow, and as darkness fell she slid away.

By the morrow, Sir Francis had organized the guard roster. The watches—of four hours, in true nautical fashion—were divided between Bertie, Aunt Florence and Hugo, so that each of them had eight hours off to sleep and to forage both for themselves and Beatrice. She, of course, could not be expected to sit unremittingly for six weeks. At least twice a day she needed to leave the egg to stretch her legs and to make herself comfortable, and at these times, usually of about a quarter of a hour's duration, Sir Francis's orders were explicit. The egg must be covered by the dodo on watch.

Aunt Florence accepted this duty without question, but it was a slightly different matter for Bertie and Hugo. Each knew that cock dodos were expected to do their fair share, but neither much wanted to—it was so boring. But Hugo did it because Aunt Florence asked him to nicely, and Bertie did it because Beatrice told him to sharply.

Sir Francis excluded himself from

the duty roster for three good reasons. Firstly, though he knew that any one of the dodos could crack a rat's head or stamp the creature flat with the utmost ease, he now doubted his own ability in single combat with his recent opponent, let alone contending with a boarding party of the pirates.

Second, he needed to exercise the gift that he alone had—of flight—to patrol the surroundings by day and give warning of danger.

Third, he was planning to kill Lucrezia Gorger.

*   *   *

Lucrezia had plans of her own.

As day succeeded day and week succeeded week, and the egg was never for a moment left unattended, so her frustration and fury grew. Every now and then Sir Francis Drake would drop down for a chat with Beatrice and whichever dodo was on watch, and on sight of him the rat's teeth chattered with rage.

'That damned parrot!' she growled to

herself. 'We'd have had that egg but for him. As it is, it must be near to hatching by now.' And then she hatched a plan.

As things stood, the egg was always covered by one or other of the great birds. She and her sons would never be able to break it. But it would be broken, and soon now! It would be broken by the chick, chipping its way out into the world. That would be the moment to attack, when the naked, new-born baby made its wobbly way out of the ruins of the egg, and its parents and probably that cursed parrot were all standing around admiring it, off their guard—then she and her boys would strike! Better still, she too would recruit reinforcements—a gang of rat-thugs to kill the chick, to kill the parrot with luck, maybe even kill the very dodos themselves!

Lucrezia Gorger shivered with blood-lust.

*   *   *

All this time Sir Francis Drake had

been observing her movements minutely. At sea he had often been accustomed to perching aloft, in the rigging or indeed in the crow's-nest, watching the seamen set sail and confusing them by shouting contrary orders in the captain's voice.

Now he sat silent in the crown of a tall palm tree and watched the rat's comings and goings. Though, of course, he had no inkling of her plans, he knew exactly the route she took each day and the position of the hiding-place from which she spied upon the rest. To reach it she had to cross an open space directly below his palm tree.

Sir Francis's plan was simple. The missile that had caused Aunt Florence to lose her memory was to cause Lucrezia Gorger to lose her life. Luck would be needed as well as very precise judgement, for Sir Francis had only one shot in his locker: a single huge coconut that hung suspended fifty feet above the centre of that open space. Each day he gnawed a little more from the stem on which the nut hung.

At last the day dawned, the scene was set. Beatrice woke to an unfamiliar sensation. Something was moving beneath her and she heard the faintest of sounds, a thin peep. Bertie chanced to be on watch and came running at her call.

Immediately, Lucrezia Gorger, watching from her hiding-place with one of her sons at her side, sent him running to fetch his brothers and the mob of twenty heavies that she had enlisted. When they arrived she issued her orders. 'Not a sound, not a movement,' she hissed, 'until I give the word.'

Aloft Sir Francis sat waiting. The coconut hung by no more than a few threads.

The minutes passed and there was no movement at the nest-site save for Bertie's nervous hopping from foot to foot. Then Beatrice stood up and moved carefully aside, and at that moment the old rat came silently out from cover and moved into the centre of the open space, the better to see the nest. The chick had hatched!

Lucrezia Gorger's beady eyes glinted, but before she could open her mouth to give the order to charge, Sir Francis Drake closed his beak and cut through the last threads that held the coconut.

CHAPTER EIGHT

A MEAL

The timing was precise, the aim perfect.

The rats were waiting, tensed for action, to hear the expected cry of 'Charge!' from Lucrezia Gorger. Instead they heard a heavy squelching thump.

High above a voice spoke words of quiet satisfaction. 'Sunk her! Split her in twain!' said the little admiral.

Presently the boldest of the Gorger boys crept forward into the open space and sniffed, hair on end, at the pancaked remains of his mother. Then with a squeal of horror he turned and dashed away, carrying the rest of the rat-gang with him in panic-stricken retreat.

Sir Francis flew down to the nest.

'Frank! Frank!' cried Beatrice in high delight. 'Look at him! Isn't he beautiful?'

Sir Francis looked at the newly hatched dodoling. In the course of a long life he had seen some ugly creatures, but never one as hideous as this. He sidestepped the question by saying 'A boy, is it?' in tones as hearty as he could manage.

'A son for my Bertie!' said Beatrice fondly. 'To carry on his name.'

'Going to call him after his father, are you?'

'Well, no, Frank,' said Bertie. 'We've just been discussing this and we thought we'd like to call him after you, seeing as you saved his life when he was a new-laid egg.'

And saved it again now he's a new-hatched chick, thought the parrot, but he did not like to spoil the parents' happy moment by revealing the terrible fate their infant had narrowly escaped.

'Call him Francis, you mean?' he said.

'Or Drake,' said Beatrice. 'You choose, Frank.'

'Well, I wouldn't pick either of them,' said Sir Francis. 'I've often thought that if I'd been lucky enough to have a son, I'd have called him either Hawkins or Frobisher.'

'Uncommon names,' said Bertie. 'Brothers of yours, perhaps?'

'Brothers-in-arms,' said Sir Francis, 'of my namesake. Fine sailors, both.'

'Oh,' said Bertie. He looked embarrassed. 'I don't really think,' he said, 'that I want my son called after a sea-monkey. Uncle Eric, you know ...' his voice trailed off.

'I'm called after a sailor,' said Sir Francis stoutly.

'Well, that's different, Frank dear,' said Beatrice. 'But it gives me an idea. Maybe something connected with your namesake might be suitable—an event or a place perhaps?'

The parrot considered this. 'If it had been a girl,' he said, 'you might have called her Armada. Wait a minute, though—a place, you said. How about naming the lad after the birthplace of the real Sir Francis Drake?'

'Where was that, Frank?' asked Bertie.

Sir Francis realized the futility of trying to explain the concept of the continent of Europe, the country of England and the county of Devonshire to two dodos who thought that their small island in the Indian Ocean was the whole world, so he simply replied, 'Tavistock. The real Sir Francis Drake was born near Tavistock. T'would make a handsome name for the lad.'

'Tavistock?' said Beatrice, thinking it over. 'I like it, don't you, Bertie?'

'It's certainly unusual,' said Bertie.

'An unusual name for an unusual child,' said Sir Francis, eyeing with distaste the bald, red, rubbery infant that was now reeling blindly about, his strangely shaped beak already open as he begged for food with hoarse squeaking sounds.

'He's hungry, bless him!' cried Beatrice. 'Bertie, go and find some food for Tavistock.'

'What sort of food, dearest?' asked Bertie. 'Something easily digested? Coconut milk perhaps?'

'No, silly,' said Beatrice. 'He needs red meat to put some feathers on his chest. Find him a nice juicy worm.'

As Bertie disappeared Aunt Florence and Hugo rolled up, and the proud mother was able to show off her child all over again. Aunt Florence was delighted with her great-nephew Tavistock.

'He has a look of his father,' she said, 'but your feet, Beatrice. As for his beak ... well, well, I declare! Who does his beak remind you of, Hugo?'

A well-shaped beak was a most important aspect of dodo beauty, and

Hugo took his cue perfectly.

'His beak,' he said, 'is indeed of a most noble shape, Florence—the very image of your own.'

And then, partly out of an enormous sense of relief that he would no longer have to stand guard (which made his varicose veins ache) or, which was worse, squat hen-like upon the egg, and partly because he felt that Beatrice had not received enough credit, he paid her the prettiest compliment he could contrive. 'I have been young and now am old,' said Hugo, 'but so lovely a mother and child I ne'er beheld in all my days!' and he gave one of his low courtly bows.

'Well spoken!' cried Aunt Florence loudly.

'Thank you,' murmured Beatrice softly.

Under his breath Sir Francis Drake let off a string of salty swearwords and flew hastily away.

★　　★　　★

Meanwhile Bertie was still searching for

a worm for Tavistock. Find him a worm, Beatrice had said, and Bertie knew better than to come back without one. He searched everywhere but there were none to be found.

Then he came to an open space directly below a tall palm tree, and in the middle of the open space was a very large coconut. Beneath the coconut was a squashed body. Bertie walked round it.

'A rat,' he said. 'And a flat rat at that.'

There was in fact little to be seen of the late Lucrezia Gorger, for her head and body were concealed by the great nut. Only one part of her stuck out—pinkish, naked, serpentine and a good nine inches long. Bertie studied the rat's tail.

'Looks like a giant worm,' he said, and he snapped it off at the root and carried it away.

Whether Beatrice would have thought it suitable was never to be known, for to ease her cramped limbs she had gone for a walk with Aunt Florence. As for Hugo, left on guard, he made off thankfully as soon as Bertie came in sight. Bertie looked fondly into the nest hollow where Tavistock lay squeaking hungrily. Carefully he

dropped his offering into the gaping mouth, and with convulsive jerks the chick, his heavy head wobbling alarmingly on his skinny neck, began to gulp it down.

Inch after inch it disappeared until finally, replete and exhausted by his efforts, Tavistock fell fast asleep. From his beak protruded still the very tip of the tail, the ultimate end of Lucrezia Gorger.

CHAPTER NINE

A CHOICE

A week after the birth of Tavistock, Fatima hatched her baby, a pretty little girl (pretty, that is, in comparison with Beatrice's hulking child) named Fancy.

The choice of this name had come about in an unplanned manner. Felix and Fatima had been discussing the matter at length and had got as far as agreeing to select four names that would do for either a girl or a boy, when a sudden tropical storm had blown up with a high wind that made it difficult for them to hear one another.

'You choose!' shouted Fatima from the nest. 'Leslie, Cecil, Hilary or Vivian?'

'Can't hear you!' bawled Felix. 'Call it whatever you fancy!' All that Fatima caught was the final word.

As soon as Fancy was fully feathered, Felix and Fatima brought her to visit Bertie and his family. Proudly each

70

mother showed off her child and praised the other's lavishly. What each said bore no relation to what she thought.

'What a lovely little girl!' said Beatrice.

(Gawky creature, she thought, coarse-featured to my mind, and I bet she's spoiled. She can't hold a candle to my Tavistock.)

'What a fine healthy boy!' said Fatima.

(Scruffy little thing, she thought, doesn't look strong, not getting enough to eat I shouldn't wonder. Not a patch on my Fancy.)

Nevertheless it was not long before they were matchmaking.

'They make a lovely couple,' said Beatrice, contemplating the two dodolings.

'Well, you never know ...' said Fatima.

'In a year or two...'

'A boy and a girl...'

'Growing up together...'

'Wouldn't it be lovely!'

'And then,' said Beatrice, 'we'd both

be grannies!'

Bertie and Felix looked at one another and rolled their eyes.

Mothers! they thought. Two chicks just out of the nest and they're marrying them off already! And by common consent they turned and walked away together.

'Let's go down to the beach,' said Beatrice.

'Yes,' said Fatima, 'the children can play on the sands.'

'Off you go then,' they said when they got there. 'Play some nice games together.'

Tavistock looked at Fancy with dislike, and Fancy looked back with distaste.

'Tavistock!' she said. 'That's a funny name.'

'So's Fancy.'

'But it's prettier. It suits me, don't you think?'

Tavistock gave a snort. 'What do you want to do?' he said.

'We could paddle,' said Fancy.

'Don't want to,' said Tavistock.

'Anyway, too much salt is bad for you, Mum says.'

'Well, race you down to the sea then.'

Tavistock looked down at Fancy. Although younger, she was already as big as him, and her legs looked particularly sturdy. She'll beat me hollow, he thought. 'Don't want to race,' he muttered, and he turned his back and slouched off. Fancy sat down in the sand and began to preen her plumage.

Bertie and Felix were having a quiet drink at the stream when Sir Francis Drake flew down to join them.

'Ahoy, me hearties!' he said, and, when he had quenched his thirst he went on, 'I wanted a word with you fellows in private.'

'What's up, Frank?' said Bertie. 'You sound very serious.'

''Tis a serious matter,' said Sir Francis. 'Come with me a moment and I'll show you what I mean.' He walked along the bank to the point where the stream emerged from the trees and ran down the beach to the ocean.

'Now,' he said, 'what do you see?'

'Dodos,' said Felix.

'But what do you notice about them in particular?'

'Well,' said Bertie, 'I notice that Beatrice and Fatima are gossiping as usual. I notice that Aunt Florence and old Hugo are standing wing to wing, looking spoony. Little Fancy is

74

preening her feathers, and Tavistock appears distinctly sulky,'

'Shiver me timbers!' cried Sir Francis. 'That's not what I mean. It's as plain as the beak on your face, if you look carefully. Your Fancy, Felix, and your Tavistock, Bertie—what are they?'

'Dodolings,' said the fathers.

'And how many other dodolings can you see on this beach?'

Bertie and Felix looked. 'Why,' said Bertie, 'hardly any! There are some bigger than our children, but none the same size, and none smaller. Yet usually the beach is covered with them. Where have all the little ones gone?'

'They never hatched,' said Sir Francis. 'The rats saw to that. You've been so taken up with your families, you two, that you haven't noticed what's going on. This island is now overrun with rats. No unguarded egg escapes them, and I've even seen them attacking newly hatched babies. They're breeding like wildfire, the rats are, but as for the dodos, there's hardly a dodoling to be seen, and soon even your children may not be safe. If things

go on as they are, with the old ones among you dying and not being replaced, it won't be long before the dodo is extinct. I warned you once before, Bertie, and you said "Dodos are forever". Remember?'

'But, Frank,' said Bertie, 'what can we do?'

'Kill the rats would be the answer,' said Sir Francis, 'if we could. But there are too many of them, and they're too quick and cunning. I was lucky to sink one.'

'Oh, it was you, was it?' said Bertie.

'Yes. But I can't drop coconuts on the lot.'

'What then?' said Felix.

'The choice is simple,' said Sir Francis. 'Before long the rats will rule the island, and sooner or later the dodos that stay here will all be dead. If you want to survive, there's only one thing for you and your families to do.'

'And what is that?' asked Bertie.

'Put to sea,' said Sir Francis Drake.

CHAPTER TEN

A BOAT

'But ... but we can't swim!' said Bertie.

'No more can I,' said Sir Francis.

'Yes, but you can fly,' said Felix.

'Not far enough.'

'Then how ...?' they said.

'Sit down, lads,' said the parrot. 'Sit ye down a while and take the weight off your feet, and listen to me. Now you must know that I wouldn't have suggested that we leave the island unless I had a plan of action. When I say "Put to sea", I mean in a boat.'

'A boat?' they said. 'What is that?'

Sir Francis realized that the word meant nothing to them. 'A wooden thing,' he explained, 'that floats on the water. The sea-monkeys came ashore in two of them, and they loaded your dead comrades into them. Remember?'

Bertie and Felix shuddered.

'How could we ever forget?' said

78

Bertie. 'But I still don't understand, Frank. We don't have one of these wooden things.'

'Ah, but there is one,' said Sir Francis, 'further along the coastline—half a day's journey perhaps. I flew over there one day not long after the typhoon, and the shore was littered with bits of wreckage that the tidal wave had washed up—spars and deck-planks and all sorts of flotsam and jetsam. And, by a miracle, one of the ship's two pinnaces was cast up on the sands just above high-water mark. I flew down and boarded her and she's as sound as a nut. No oars of course—they'd been washed away. Still, none of us can row. But if there was room aboard for eight oarsmen and a helmsman, then there's room for eight dodos and a green parrot. So what say you, my lads? Shall we put to sea and sail away over the ocean wave?'

Bertie and Felix did not answer. The whole idea was so foreign to them—the thought of themselves and Beatrice and Fatima and little Fancy and young Tavistock and old Hugo and Aunt

Florence sailing away under the command of Sir Francis Drake. Surely there was no immediate danger. Why need they leave the island?

The answer came with dramatic suddenness.

While Sir Francis had been talking to the two cock dodos, Beatrice and Fatima had walked down to the sea for a paddle. Tavistock mooched along behind them, sulking because his mother had told him off for not playing nicely with Fancy. She still sat alone at the top of the beach, prinking herself, when suddenly a positive army of rats appeared.

Stealthily, silently, like a grey blanket on the golden sands, they advanced towards the unsuspecting dodoling. They were almost upon her before she saw them.

'Help!' screamed Fancy, and 'Daddy's coming, baby!' yelled Felix, and 'Get away, you brutes!' shouted Bertie as they pounded to the rescue.

As for Sir Francis, he flew at the rats making ear-splitting cries. 'Avast, ye murdering sons of sea-cooks!' he

screeched, and at the sound, and at the sight of the great dodos thundering towards them, the rats hesitated, snarling and squealing, and then broke and ran. A few of the boldest leaped at

81

the terrified Fancy, only to die before the stabbing beaks or beneath the stamping feet of the furious cocks.

Soon the rest came running. 'Are you all right, darling?' cried Fatima to her daughter.

'Why can't you do what you're told?' said Beatrice to her son.

'Never mind, dear,' said Aunt Florence to her great-nephew.

Hugo, arriving last, lunged fiercely at a limp grey body. 'How now! A rat,' he cried, 'dead for a ducat, dead!'

Still panting from their exertions, Bertie and Felix looked at one another and then at Sir Francis. 'That settles it,' they said. 'We'll take our chance at sea.'

'Well spoken, lads!' cried the parrot. 'Cast off then, and follow me! Never fear a voyage to take, put your faith in old Frank Drake!'

'Come on then, all of you,' said Bertie. 'Follow Frank.'

'Why should we?' said Beatrice.

'Why can't you do what you're told?' said Bertie to his wife, and Tavistock smiled happily to himself.

On Sir Francis's instructions, the eight dodos set out to walk along the beach at the sea's edge.

''Tis a longer route,' said the parrot, 'but easier for the littl'uns than struggling across country.'

In the interior of the island, he thought, among the thick tropical vegetation, they would be in constant danger of ambush from the rats. But out in the open they could not be surprised, and it would take a bold band of the brutes to face six angry adult dodos.

So Sir Francis flew ahead, for his walking pace was terribly slow, while the dodos tramped along the coastline, following him. Every now and then he would wait for them to catch up, and every now and then he climbed high into the sky to look for danger.

Once he saw, in a clearing in the trees, a swarm of rats feasting on the carcass of some animal. He swooped low over them, while they yakkered and chittered with rage at him, and saw that they were eating a dead dodo. Died of old age, I dare say, he said to himself as he flew away, but something told him that that might not have been the cause of death, and he urged his friends to make haste.

By nightfall they had still not sighted the boat, and they rested a while for the two dodolings were tired and footsore. The adults formed a ring around Tavistock and Fancy facing outwards, and though they could hear squeakings and scurryings in the darkness, the rats were not yet ready to face those six great beaks. Then the moon rose and they pressed on once more.

It was a brilliant full moon, which lit the shore so brightly that Sir Francis was able to fly by its light, and soon he came hurrying back with good news.

'Nearly there, me hearties!' he cried. 'She's just around the next headland.'

And, sure enough, it was not long before the dodos sighted the ship's boat. The pinnace lay on the sand just above the high-tide mark, bows to sea, and the birds gathered round and looked anxiously at it.

'We can get into it all right, Frank,' said Bertie, 'but how do we get it into the sea?'

'You won't need to lift a wing, Bertie,' said Sir Francis. 'The sea will do the work for us. These are spring tides when the water comes furthest up the beach, and tonight it just so happens—if my reckoning's correct (and old Frank Drake knows the ways of the sea)—tonight at the full of the moon, it will be the highest tide of the whole year. We're just in time. Another hour, and she'd have floated away. So it's all aboard, shipmates—handsomely now!'

Somehow the clumsy dodos tumbled in over the gunwales of the pinnace and perched themselves upon the thwarts, while Sir Francis Drake took his place in the stern. All of them stared at the line of ripples that the tide was bringing nearer, until they felt the slightest of shudders as a wave broke against the prow of the boat.

So intent were they on watching the sea's approach that none looked behind, where a thousand eyes were glinting in the light of the rising moon.

CHAPTER ELEVEN

A VOYAGE

Lucrezia Gorger had not lived in vain, for although she did not bequeath all her ferocity and cunning to her five sons, they none the less had inherited a good measure of both.

After their mother's death they had separated, each moving to a different part of the island and each fighting his way to become leader or king rat of perhaps a hundred of his fellows. Each Gorger boy kept to his own territory and respected that of his brothers', for there was plenty of food for all.

The staple of their diet was of course the great egg of the dodo. The Gorgers had invented new and more efficient ways to break the egg, such as manoeuvring it to the foot of a low cliff and then pushing rocks off the top to smash it. Soon they had progressed to killing newly hatched chicks, and then quite sizeable dodolings. And (as Sir

Francis had seen) they had now graduated to pulling down elderly or sick adults.

When the eldest Gorger boy, whose territory was nearest to Bertie and Beatrice's home-beach, saw the six adults and two dodolings set out on their long march, he summoned his band and followed, at first out of mere curiosity. But as the travellers made their way further round the shoreline, the first Gorger crossed into the territory of the second, whose band then joined the pursuit. Messengers were sent to the other three brothers, and by the time that Sir Francis and his friends had reached the pinnace five hundred rats had massed, waiting and watching and working themselves up to a new pitch of boldness.

The Gorger boys held a council of war.

'Forget the parrot,' said one. 'His squawk is worse than his bite.'

'Forget the two dodolings,' said the second. 'They're easy meat.'

'Forget the two old birds,' said the third. 'They're tired out.'

'That' said the fourth, 'leaves us only four dodos to deal with. Four against five hundred.'

'And beyond them is the sea,' said the eldest Gorger. 'There's no escape for them; nowhere for them to go.'

'Except down our throats!' growled his brothers.

If only Ma were here to see this!' said the eldest Gorger. 'Back to your troops, boys, and wait for my word!'

He gave the word—the squeal of 'Charge!' that Lucrezia Gorger had not had time to utter—just as the seventh and biggest wave of the highest spring tide of the year lifted the pinnace from its resting-place and, drawing back again, pulled it into the shallows. As the attackers came racing down the beach another wave, and another, and another, dragged the boat further and further away from the sands, covered now with a host of chattering, squeaking, furious, frustrated rats. The tide turned and the ebb began, and Sir Francis Drake and his crew sailed steadily out to sea.

'A near-run thing, ye might say,' said

the little admiral drily.

Except for Tavistock and Fancy who were no sooner aboard than they had fallen fast asleep from exhaustion, not knowing anything of the danger, the dodos were effusive in their relief.

'Did you see them!' said Beatrice.

'Hundreds and hundreds of them!' said Fatima.

'We could never have fought off so many!' said Hugo.

'What an escape!' said Felix.

'And all due to our noble Sir Francis!' said Aunt Florence.

'Yes,' said Bertie soberly, 'we owe you our lives, Frank. But what now? Where are we going?'

'The answer to that, Bertie,' said Sir Francis, 'I don't rightly know. But what I hope is that with the help of wind and current and a generous tot of luck, we shall find ourselves another island.'

'There are other islands?'

'Dozens of them in this part of the world. Some maybe as big as yours, some much smaller. Some are known to the sea-monkeys, as you call them, but many are not. We must hope to find such a one.'

'But how are we to survive, Frank?' asked Beatrice. 'What are we to eat and drink?'

'Let us worry about that tomorrow,' said the parrot. 'For now, rest and sleep. We've a dry night and a fair wind and your captain's at the helm.'

★　　★　　★

When morning broke they woke to find that the current had carried them far from land. Whichever way the dodos looked, there was nothing but water and more water as far as the eye could see. The sun rose sharply in the sky and blazed down upon the voyagers, and the dodolings began to grizzle.

'I'm hot!' wailed Fancy and 'I'm hungry!' whined Tavistock and 'We're thirsty!' they whimpered. 'And we feel sick!'

Even the adults began to grumble. 'I can't see any of your "dozens of islands", Frank,' aid Beatrice pettishly.

By midday morale among Sir

Francis's crew was low, as all the birds lay gasping in the well of the pinnace, their little wings outspread, their big beaks agape.

The parrot set himself to cheer them up. 'Y'know,' he said, 'the real Sir Francis Drake fought against the Spaniards.'

'What are they?' panted Bertie.

'A different kind of sea-monkey. And my namesake always seemed to know just where their ships were. The Spaniards believed that he had a magic mirror in his cabin, so that he could see right over the horizon. Now, I've no magic mirror, but I can see beyond the horizon if I fly high enough.'

'You're not leaving us, Sir Francis?' said Aunt Florence anxiously.

'Calm yourself, ma'am,' said the parrot, 'I'm just going aloft to see what I can see. I'll be back afore you can say "Plymouth Hoe".' He took off and climbed steeply into the cloudless sky.

His return roused the dodos from their lethargy, but alas he had nothing to report but the promise of a change in the weather, for from his vantage point he had seen angry clouds building up afar.

'Not another typhoon?' cried Beatrice fearfully.

'Bless you, no,' said Sir Francis cheerfully. 'A tropical squall, no more, and we'll be glad of it, mark my words.'

And indeed they were glad, for when the squall struck it brought a sudden deluge of rain that cooled their baked bodies. Then it was gone again, leaving a great pool of water in the bottom of the boat so that all could quench their thirst.

As an added bonus the passage of the squall seemed to excite a large shoal of flying fish, which leaped from the surface of the sea, their flashing, rainbow-hued bodies skimming along above the waves. A score or more actually hurled themselves into the pinnace and the dodos feasted on them.

So by nightfall everyone had had plenty to eat and drink. The sun sank beneath the waves, taking its terrible heat with it. Sir Francis sang them a number of rousing sea-shanties, and everyone began to feel that tomorrow would bring the sanctuary that they sought.

But the morrow came and went without a glimpse of land, and the next day, and the next. Twice a rainstorm swept over them and a few more flying-fish jumped aboard, but by the

fifth day all were growing weak. The end, it seemed was near.

There were other creatures that sensed this for a number of large shapes cruised around the pinnace, their triangular dorsal fins sticking black and threatening above the surface. The sharks circled ever closer and one even bumped the boat with his broad snout.

Sir Francis looked around at his companions, sprawled about in listless attitudes. He cast a weather eye up at the sky and scanned the rim of his world as he had done a hundred times a day. By now he had given up his reconnaissance flights; he did not feel up to them.

And then suddenly 'LAND HO!' screeched Sir Francis Drake.

'What? croaked the dodos.

'Land two points on the larboard bow! I saw it just now, on the lift of a wave! There! There 'tis again! We've made a landfall, shipmates—d'ye see it now?'

All struggled to their feet and stared, and there on the horizon, sure enough, was a small dark shape that gradually became larger and more defined as they sailed on, until they could actually see the whiteness of breaking waves and beyond, the green of trees.

The dodos were noisily ecstatic, all their hunger and thirst and exhaustion forgotten. They had lost their earthly paradise to the forces of evil, but here was another one!

Only Sir Francis sat silent and watchful, knowing that they were far from home and dry. Captain he might be, but where wind and current should take his command was in the lap of the gods of the sea. If they so decreed, the pinnace would sail straight past and away again into the watery wastes.

But the gods were kind.

As they drew steadily nearer, Sir Francis could see that this was no ordinary island. Around it, some distance from its shores, was a coral atoll, a circular ring of rock, and within the ring was a great lagoon, and within the lagoon was the island itself.

Perfect! thought Sir Francis. No ship would try to land here and risk holing herself or her boats on those jagged rocks. Then he saw that there was a narrow gap in the coral ring, a gap through which the incoming tide was boiling, a gap towards which the pinnace was even now being sucked, faster and faster.

For a moment it seemed that they would slip neatly through the opening, but at the last moment an eddy in the racing tide caught the boat and turned it sideways. There was a rending crash as the razor-sharp coral ripped open the boat's side and the sea began to pour in.

'Abandon ship!' yelled Sir Francis Drake. 'Women and children first!'

The dodos stared about in confusion. Under them the pinnace was rapidly filling. Before them lay the lagoon, a wide stretch of water between them and dry land. Behind them they could see as they looked fearfully back those black triangular fins cruising to and fro.

'Stir your stumps!' shouted Sir Francis. 'She's going down! You must swim for it—work your legs as if you were running, you'll be all right. Jump, Beatrice! Jump, Fatima! And you, Aunt Florence, ma'am! And you littl'uns, climb on your mothers' backs!'

So the three hens jumped overboard, and Tavistock and Fancy scrambled upon their mothers, and, once they were clear of the boat, Bertie and Felix and Hugo followed.

All struck out madly, flapping their useless little wings and kicking with their great feet, and at first they made some progress. However, they did not help themselves by continually glancing back in terror, not knowing that the sharks never came through the narrow gap into the lagoon. But gradually, as their feathers grew sodden, they began to sink.

Sir Francis Drake sat on the tiller, watching. By tradition the captain must always be the last to leave his ship, and anyway there was nothing he could do for the dodos now. Slowly, he could see, they were settling lower and lower, until only six big heads and two little ones stuck out above the surface.

'Farewell, shipmates,' muttered the parrot, and then to his amazement and relief he saw the heads beginning to rise. The dodos had reached the shallows of the lagoon and had struck bottom. Eagerly they stumbled ashore and collapsed on the beach, worn out, soaked through, but safe.

With a last gurgle, the wrecked pinnace slipped beneath the water, and Sir Francis flew to join his friends.

CHAPTER TWELVE

A GRANDCHILD

How nice it would be to say that they all lived happily ever after. But 'ever' expects too much, for all dodos, like all people (and all parrots), must one day die. If illness or accident or such a fate as overtook Bertie's poor Uncle Eric does not carry them off, then old age will.

But Sir Francis and his friends did indeed live happily for a good long time, for the island on which they had happened was all that they could have hoped for. There was fresh water to drink and fine trees for shelter and plenty to eat—plants and fruit and a good selection of seafood. And there were no rats!

There were no other dodos either, but it was not long before their numbers began to increase. Soon after the landing, once they were rested and had recovered from their ordeal, Sir

Francis was called upon to perform a very pleasant duty; nothing less than the marriage of Aunt Florence to the elderly but well-preserved Hugo. And not long after that—to everyone's surprise—Aunt Florence proceeded to lay an egg and in due course to hatch out a dear little chick, the apple of her ageing parents' eyes.

As for the younger dodos, each pair produced a chick each year and, by a happy chance, if Beatrice had a daughter, Fatima would have a son,

and vice versa, so that by the time the last of the dodos on their old island had fallen to the rats, there was a plentiful supply of dodolings on Drakeland. This was what the birds called their new home, in honour of their saviour, and one of the last pleasures of his long life was to be present at the birth of the first grandson of Beatrice and Bertie and Fatima and Felix.

In youth Tavistock and Fancy had had little to do with one another, but there came a day when Tavistock looked at the eldest daughter of Felix and Fatima and saw that she had grown into a beautiful bird, and his heart swelled in his breast.

And Fancy's heart fluttered in her bosom as she looked back at Bertie and Beatrice's eldest son. Love at first sight you could not have called it, but love at last it was; and so old Sir Francis married them, and they hatched a fine boy whom they called after Grandpa Bertie's real name, Eggbert.

In due course each of Bertie and Beatrice's many sons and daughters grew up and, quite naturally, chose as wife or husband one of Felix and Fatima's equally huge family; and more babies were born to grown into dodolings, and eventually to become parents themselves.

Of course there was a variety of names that were chosen for Drakeland chicks (including, I'm glad to say, several called Eric), but certain ones always remained the most popular, and there was never any lack of Berties and Beatrices, Felixes, Fatimas, Florences and Hugos.

And as the years and the decades and the centuries went by, mothers still told their children the old stories—of the sea-monkeys and the rats, of the eight brave voyagers, and of their captain, the green parrot called Sir Francis Drake.

POSTSCRIPT

One day two young dodos stood side by side on the beach on Drakeland. The date (though they did not know this) was AD 2000, three hundred and fifty years after the start of this story.

The world had changed enormously, but they and their kind had not altered in the slightest. Heavy, awkward and clumsy, they stood wing to wing, and one (whose name chanced to be Bertie) said, 'How about getting married?' and the other (whose name happened to be Beatrice) replied, 'What a good idea.'

So remember, when people tell you (as they will) 'The dodo is extinct', to allow yourself a small smile.

For now you know (and don't ever tell anyone else) that on a little island somewhere in the Indian Ocean, dodos are forever.